Pat and the Gabby Goats

Diane Odegard Gockel

Dedication

To my friend Barbara, the Goat Lady, who has dedicated her life to rescuing and finding new homes for goats. To our son Tom, one of the best thinkers I know. Your belly laugh and sense of humor are a joy to be around. We love you. And to Pat, the eldest goat, we have so enjoyed you on our farm, big boy.

About the Author

Diane Odegard Gockel is a former high school teacher who has devoted much of her life to the rescue, fostering, and adoption of homeless pets. She and her daughter, Julie Diane Stafford, co-own Unplug and Create. Diane and her husband have four grown children and live on a small farm in Sammamish, Washington, called Second Chance Ranch.

Other Books in the Rescue Series by
Diane Odegard Gockel

The Rescue of Winks
Bella Saves the Farm
Al the Alpaca: Forever Friends
Fancy Has a Plan

Pat and the Gabby Goats

I am Patrick the goat, one of the oldest animals living on Second Chance Ranch. I am one of those lucky pets that was rescued and brought here to live with and be loved by the Farm Lady, Farm Man, and their four children.

I was born at a roadside farmers' market and fruit stand. The store owners had several farm animals on display on the premises to attract potential buyers driving by. My mom told me families would stop to pet the farm animals and oftentimes would buy some pie, jam, or fresh fruits. This was great during the summer, but during the off-season, the store would close, and many times the owners neglected to feed us on a regular basis, and no families came to visit. I was born during the off-season.

My sister was brown like Mama, and I was pure white. We were all very hungry. I was about two weeks old when I first met the Farm Lady. I was surprised to see anyone on the farm since the stores were all closed, but clearly she came just to see the animals. She was with her two sons.

"Oh, you poor thing!" the Farm Lady said to my mama as her sons entered our pens to play with us. "You look so hungry! If I take one of your babies with me, Mama, you will have enough food to feed the other."

The Farm Lady went up and knocked on the door of the farmhouse, and after a brief conversation with the woman in the house, she came back and scooped me up in her arms and carried me to her car. I sat on the boys' laps, hungry and very tired.

We made one quick stop on the way home, and the Farm Lady bought milk—lots of milk! When we reached the farm, her sons took me out to a little pasture and sat me on top of a picnic table. Minutes later, the Farm Lady entered the pasture with a large bottle of something and offered it to me. As soon as I latched onto the bottle, I could feel and taste the warmth of sweet goat's milk.

I began to drink and drink as the Farm Lady held the bottle upside down for me. It reminded me of Mama, only this milk didn't run out!

"That's enough now, or you will get a tummy ache!" she laughed. "I will name you Patrick, as it is St. Patrick's Day weekend."

Not only was I given a name, I was also given a home. As I grew up that summer, I began to search my surroundings, and I realized that I was not the only goat on the farm. There were two very old goats that taught me a lot, and I started to follow them everywhere. Buddy was a tan goat with darker ears, and Munch was a short, fat goat and all black. They taught me how to keep the two border collies from chasing me and that it was better to leave the two horses alone. I learned all I could from these two very old goats, and my heart felt empty in the year ahead when they both passed away from old age.

The Farm Lady knew that goats are herd animals and do not like to live alone, so she was determined to find me a friend. She went to see her friend the Goat Lady, at the local shelter, and brought back four goats. Bailey was a silly-looking brown-and-white adult goat with ears that stuck straight out from the sides of his head like wings. Daisy was a black goat that never had her horns removed as a kid, and she was very proud of them. Then there were the very young gabby goats, twins that were all white (like me), but silly and chatty. Their names were Huckleberry and Loganberry, but we just called them Huck and Logan.

Huckleberry and Loganberry never stopped talking and never listened to a word we said. They were constantly getting chased by the border collies and always got caught in the rain. The most annoying thing about Huck and Logan was they never followed me as the senior goat. I overheard them once say that they didn't need to listen to the old goat. Bailey and Daisy followed me around the pasture and were interested in what I had to say, but Huck and Logan were always doing their own thing and getting themselves into trouble.

One afternoon, after several hours of grazing, I said to Bailey and Daisy, "We better head back up to the barn; I feel a storm coming on."

"How do you know, Pat?" questioned Bailey.

"Listen…Hear the stillness in the air? Notice the darker sky and the wind that is coming from that direction? Then, smell the air, and you will feel the storm in your bones, and you will know to head back. Practice this and notice these things, and you will know when the weather is changing."

Soon after we headed to the barn, the rain started to pound the barn roof and the pasture grass. The wind picked up, and the rain started to blow sideways. I looked out the barn door for Huck and Logan. Off at the very end of the pasture, I spotted them, looking scared and lost.

Huck and Logan were soaking wet with their heads drooped to avoid the rain and wind on their faces. They were clearly having a hard time finding their way back to the barn.

"If they had been following us, this would not be happening," Daisy explained as she peeked out the barn door with me.

"I must go get them," I said as I galloped out the barn door before Daisy could protest.

The rain was heavy, and the wind blew hard at my side. Huck and Logan seemed to be making little to no progress toward safety. I pushed toward the two gabby goats with determination, remembering why goats dislike the rain so much. I was angry with them for not following along, but for now, I had to get them to the safety of the barn. The Farm Lady loved the twins, and I needed to protect them. As I finally reached them, they both looked up in surprise and with fear in their eyes.

"Patrick! Help!" cried Logan.

"We can't see the barn!" added Huck.

"Listen!" I commanded. "Follow me! Stay close behind. Huck, keep your head close to my right back leg, and it will protect you. You can also see where I am leading you without having to look up too much. Logan, you do the same with Huck. Stay close!"

They both seemed to understand and followed without objection. As we reached the barn door, both the gabby goats bolted in and began to shake and shiver. No one said a word as we watched the storm pass through. Even the gabby goats were silent.

After a little while, the sky began to turn blue again, and the winds died down to stillness. Out the barn door, you could see the horses in the adjacent pasture heading out from their barn to graze again. I nodded to Daisy, and we headed out the barn door to nibble on some rich green grass before nightfall.

As I was grazing, I kept feeling something bumping up against my tail and back leg. Looking back, I could see Huck and Logan following close behind. That afternoon they said very little and followed me, observing everything I did. I smiled inside.

It was Huck who finally broke his silence. "Pat? Why do the border collies chase Logan and me, but they never chase you?"

"Because you run from them," I explained. "Chase and Bella will never hurt you. It's just a game for them. Next time they run after you, don't run, and they will stop chasing you."

At that moment, I remembered Buddy and Munch and how good they were to me. I also recalled that I, too, was a gabby little goat as a kid and how patient Buddy and Munch were when I wouldn't listen to or follow their great wealth of advice. I guess we learn only when we are ready.

"Come on, Huck and Logan! I'm going to show you where the best blackberries are!" I said as we trotted to the back side of the barn.

"I've never had blackberries!" squealed Huck with delight.

"Oh, you will love them!" I affirmed.

As the three of us munched away at the berries, I realized that I really did like these gabby goats. And Huck learned that he loves blackberries, too, but if you eat too many, you get a tummy ache.

I have had twelve summers here on the farm. Last year, we got to share our pasture with Al the alpaca and his friends. And this summer, the Farm Lady added two new rescue goats, Dahlia and Daphne (she likes to name the girl goats after the flowers in her garden).

As the seasons pass and I feel myself getting older, I often worry about how well the other goats would do when I pass away.

This morning, I started to think to myself that it might rain and I should tell the others to head for the barn. Before I could get the message out, Huck came running up to Daphne and Dahlia and proclaimed, "I think it might rain! We should head to the barn! Hurry!"

As I felt a few drops of rain hit my back as I entered the barn, I thought about how Huck and Logan had become great leaders.

It seems my job now is just to relax and enjoy my last summers on Second Chance Ranch.

The Real Patrick the Goat

Huck and Logan

The Whole Gang

Made in the USA
Coppell, TX
12 August 2020